FAN LETTERS

...I love books and animals, so your book combined my two favorite things. I definitely will be reading the other books in this series! (Taylor S. in Arizona)

...I love the CCSC! My favorite character is Kelsey Case because she loves to spy, is always ready to solve a mystery and she can lip-read.
(Addison age 10)

REVIEWS

...three youngsters work together with the common goal of helping animals—and end up learning the true meaning of friendship.
 (**Kind News,** THE HUMANE SOCIETY of the United States)

...There's plenty of action in this series opener but Singleton also handles the emotional layers well. Pet lovers will enjoy the animal-centric focus, and the mystery will keep them guessing.
 (**Publishers Weekly**)

....This enjoyable mystery has a satisfying ending and a neatly calibrated level of suspense for middle school readers. (**Kirkus Reviews**)

...A fun mystery series that's a sure bet for animal lovers. (**School Library Journal**)

DOG RESCUE

TIME WARP

A CCSC Mini Mystery

Starring

DOG RESCUE TIME WARP

A CURIOUS CAT SPY CLUB Mini-Mystery

by Linda Joy Singleton

"According to my calculations, we'll find a new mystery today," Leo says, staring at the Skunk Shack door like he expects it to burst open.

I arch my brow. "How do you figure that?"

"Isn't it obvious, Kelsey?" He pushes back his blond hair as he continues to watch the door." I've analyzed the statistics and on average we encounter a mystery every 2.4 weeks."

Becca rolls her eyes and I try not to giggle. We're sitting at the lopsided table we found when we cleaned the Skunk Shack and formed the Curious Cat Spy Club. Leo is our Covert Technology Strategist, Becca is our Social Contact Operative and I'm the Spy Tactics Specialist. We're 7th graders at Helen

Corning Middle School but we didn't become friends until we rescued three kittens from a dumpster and tracked down the person who dumped them. Now we meet after school and sometimes on weekends to solve animal mysteries.

"Mysteries don't follow a schedule like school holidays," Becca tells Leo with a flip of her pink-streaked ponytail.

I nod. "You can't just expect one to show up at our clubhouse."

At that moment there's a scratching sound on the door.

Leo jumps up and opens the door—and finds a reddish-brown dog with a bloody front paw.

****

The dog is a mess!

Her fur is wet, mud-splattered and tangled with burrs. Muddy prints trail on the floor as she staggers into the room, panting as if she's been running for miles.

Becca rushes over to the injured dog. "Poor puppy!"

"The dog is fully grown, clearly not a puppy," Leo points out.

"She's in trouble and needs help." I rip off a paper towel and hand it to Becca. "Here."

Becca kneels beside the dog, speaking gently as she examines the bloody paw. "Hmm...that's weird."

"What?" Leo asks.

"She has blood on her paw but she's not bleeding and there are no cuts."

Leo taps his chin thoughtfully. "So whose blood is it?"

"No idea." Becca shrugs.

"Poor thing is exhausted." I pour her a bowl of water and set it down.

"This is very mysterious," Leo says as we watch the dog lap water. "A bloody paw but no injuries. And how did she get wet? The stream running through the woods is dry."

"Bird Lake still has water." Becca points in the direction of Wild Oaks Animal Sanctuary where she and her mother live with a menagerie of rescued animals.

"There isn't any bird goo or feathers on her fur," Leo points out.

"Wow! Look at the size of this burr." I gently pry a prickly burr from the dog's fur. "I've never seen one this big."

"Not around here," Becca agrees. "This dog must have traveled a long distance. What does her tag say?"

The dog's fur is so thick I hadn't noticed the tag. But now I see a silver glint from a dangling bone-shaped tag. I squint at the tiny inscription. "Her name is Sandy. She lives in Sun Flower on Myrtle Avenue. There's a phone number, too."

"Sorry Leo, but there's no mystery to solve." Becca says with a gentle smile. "Sandy is just a lost dog."

"Not for long," I add, jiggling the collar tags.

"I'll call Sandy's owner." Becca slips her phone from her pocket. She taps the screen and listens a moment. Her smile fades to a frown. "The number doesn't work."

"I'll look up the address." Leo checks his phone then frowns. "According to my map search, Myrtle Avenue doesn't exist in Sun Flower."

I wrinkle my brow. "But she has to live around here somewhere."

"I'll implement a more detailed search in media and images," Leo says, tapping on his phone. After a few seconds, he looks up with a puzzled expression. "I found the house...but this can't be right."

I peer over Leo's shoulder at a photo of a rectangular house with an attached garage and neatly mowed front yard. The house is on a corner with oak trees rising in the distance. Two kids about our age sit on the cement steps beneath a covered porch; an auburn-haired girl with brown-framed glasses and a boy with wavy brown hair and a friendly grin.

The girl has her arm around the dog in our photo.

"Great work." I grin at Leo. "You found Sandy's owners."

Leo shakes his head. "It can't be the same dog."

"It's the same red collar." Becca points. "Of course it's Sandy."

"Impossible." Leo goes pale. "This photo was taken 47 years ago."

****

Becca and I stare at Leo like he has suddenly grown a tail and is barking in dog language.

"You're joking...right?" I ask uneasily.

"When have I ever told a joke?" Leo says with zero humor.

"But you can't be serious." Becca pushes wispy strands of dark hair away from her eyes.

I nod. "Or Sandy would be 50 years old--the oldest living dog ever!"

"I didn't say I believed the factuality of this photo," Leo lifts his chin. "If it's not a fabrication then the date is an error. The dog in the photograph is most likely an ancestor of Sandy's. The important fact is that this photo proves Sandy's address is legitimate. It shouldn't be too difficult to find its location."

"But not tonight," Becca says with a gesture to the dusky sky. "It's getting late."

"Yeah." I glance at my watch. "I have to go home for dinner."

"I propose we reconvene at my house in the morning," Leo suggests.

"Sounds like a plan," Becca says, and I nod.

Before we leave, we gather clues from Sandy. Using tweezers, Leo plucks burrs, mud and other particles from Sandy's fur. I zip the clues into an "evidence" baggie. Becca offers to bathe Sandy and keep her overnight. I'll check with my Animal Control Officer mother for a missing pet report on Sandy.

In the morning Becca and I roll up to Leo's house at the same time.

"It wasn't easy riding here with Sandy tugging on her leash," Becca says as she slides off her bike. "She runs faster than I can pedal."

"She's eager to go home." I stroke her reddish-brown fur which is now silky smooth from being washed and brushed. "But none of Mom's lost dog reports match."

"So how do we find her home?" Becca's beaded bracelets jingle as she spreads out her arms. "Sandy wouldn't sleep last night, pacing my room and whining at the door."

"I have the solution." Leo steps out of his house holding his gyro-boar, a speedy robotic skateboard. "Myrtle Avenue wasn't on recent maps but I found it on an old one. It's in south east Sun Flower, near the freeway."

"I didn't think there were homes in that area, just warehouses," I say, puzzled. "And why is the address only on an old map?"

"We'll find out when we get there." He holds out his hand to Becca. "I'll take Sandy's leash so she can guide us."

Leo zooms ahead on his gyro-board, holding Sandy's leash while Becca and I pedal fast to keep up with them. We weave through a new subdivision then bump along a rutted road until we reach an industrial warehouse area with trash blown against fences. Sandy bounds across a cracked-cement lot, stopping abruptly at a chain-link fence bordering the busy freeway.

I slow my bike beside my friends. "Why did Sandy stop here?"

Leo checks his phone. He looks around, frowning. "According to my calculations, Myrtle Avenue should be on the other side of this fence."

"But it isn't," Becca says in a disappointed tone. "There aren't any houses."

"Only the freeway." I raise my voice to be heard over the rushing traffic.

"Sandy, don't jerk the leash!" Leo struggles to hold the dog while balancing on his gyro-board.

"Why is she trying to get to the freeway?" I wonder.

"She's confused." Becca sighs. "Poor lost doggie. She doesn't know how to get home."

"Or she knows something we don't." Leo points at a faded street sign sticking up in the corner of the fence.

Myrtle Avenue.

Suddenly Sandy lunges toward the fence, dragging her leash and Leo. She springs into the air and leaps at the street sign. Leo shouts for her to stop but his words are cut off as both boy and dog vanish.

Becca and I drop our bikes. We run forward. My sneakers pound on pavement and my brain screams, "Impossible! Turn around!"

But it's like I'm being sucked into an invisible tornado. My head spins. My feet pound faster and faster as if I'm running on air. Becca is ahead of me then suddenly she's not there.

I'm screaming, scared but unable to stop running.

And then I'm somewhere else.

****

I'm lying on hard pavement, a wet dog tongue slurping my face.

"Sandy, stop," I push the dog away and grab hold of a wooden post to ease myself up.

Glancing around, I'm relieved to see Becca and Leo staggering to their feet, too.

Becca rubs her head. "What happened?"

"Um...was I flying?" Leo blinks in confusion. "Where are we?"

Dizzily, I look up at the wooden post I grabbed. Not a post, but the Myrtle Avenue sign--except it's no longer faded a dingy gray. Instead, it's bright white with bold black lettering.

Leo picks up his gyro-board, looking even more confused than I feel. "Where did the fence go?"

"That's not all that's missing." Becca gestures around us. "The freeway is gone!"

The busy world of traffic has been clicked off like the power button on a remote. I take a deep breath of sweet flowery air and glance up at birds flittering from shady treetops. Everything seems normal, yet somehow different.

"Where did these homes come from?" I peer down a street of single-story homes in pastel greens, browns and blues. Each house has an attached garage, a neatly mowed front yard with blooming flower beds, and one or two classic cars in the driveway.

"I have a theory," Leo says in a solemn tone.

"Good because I'm tilting on the edge of crazy." Becca twists the end of her ponytail.

"Something weird is definitely going on." I shiver, longing for the familiar roar of traffic. "What's your theory?"

"We're suffering from mass hallucinations," Leo answers. "It's the only logical explanation."

I can think of another explanation—but it's even crazier.

Sandy barks and takes off down the street, her leash clattering behind her on the pavement.

"Catch that dog!" I shout as I start to run. "All this weirdness started with Sandy. We can't lose her!"

Leo zooms ahead on his gyro-board. Houses blur by and I glimpse a few kids playing in their yards. I'm running so fast my side aches. Finally, Sandy turns into a driveway at the end of the street. She scampers up the front porch of a green house.

The house from the photo!

And the girl and boy rushing over to Sandy are from the photo, too!

"Sandy! We're been calling all over for you! Where have you been?" The auburn-haired girl cries as she hugs the dog. The boy—probably her younger brother—hugs Sandy, too.

Leo, Becca and I exchange puzzled, "how is this possible?" looks.

"Thanks for bringing Sandy home." The girl waves us over. We hesitate then cautiously walk up to the porch. "Eddie and I have been really worried because she didn't come home last night."

"Lu was afraid Sandy was lost," the brown-haired boy—Eddie—says. "But Sandy is too smart for that."

"Even a smart dog can get lost," Becca says, bending over to pet Sandy. "She showed up at our clubhouse and was such a mess that we thought she'd been in an accident. But she didn't have any injuries. She stayed the night at my house and I gave her a bath."

"You did a super job!" Lu pushes up her brown glasses as she sniffs Sandy's fur. "Her fur shines and she smells pretty, like peaches."

"It's a new canine shampoo my mom ordered online," Becca says.

"Online?" Lu scrunches her brows. "Never heard of that catalog. My mother only orders encyclopedias through the mail."

"And the Happy Hollister books," her brother adds. "I liked the *Mystery at Missile Town* best. My friend and I are going to build a rocket to the moon."

"Ignore my brother." Lu rolls her dark eyes. "He's been crazy about space travel since watching the moonwalk. Everyone knows kids can't be astronauts."

"I can if I want," Eddie retorts. "But you can't because you're a girl."

I glance over at Leo, expecting him to correct Eddie and recite names, facts and dates about the first woman astronaut. But Leo is unusually quiet. He stares at Eddie and Lu like he's calculating a difficult math equation.

Something about these kids doesn't add up. They seem…I don't know…different.

I slip into "spy" mode and study them. Lu's polka-dotted cotton blouse has a ruffle around the bottom like a toddler would wear. Her sneakers are plain white with no brand logo and her white socks go up to her knees. Eddie wears a striped buttoned-up shirt and brown corduroy pants. One of his white sneaker laces is broken and flops as he walks.

His brown hair is short except for a wavy curl over his brown eyes—just like the photo.

They seem to be curious about us, too.

"I haven't seen you at school." Eddie squints. "Are you new to Sun Flower?"

I shake my head. "I've lived here since I was little."

Eddie scratches his chin. "I know all the kids around here but I've never seen you before."

"They probably go to St. Agnes Academy," Lu says.

I've never heard of that school, and my club mates look confused, too. Leo arches his brows. "Where is it located?"

"On Sycamore Street," Lu answers. "You know, next to the olive orchard."

"Actually I don't know. But I can find out." Leo tilts his head in his "thinking" pose and he pulls his cell from his pocket. He taps his phone then frowns. "No signal."

Becca checks her phone. "Me, neither."

They don't ask me because I don't have a phone. As the youngest of four kids in a family with a tight budget, I'll be grown with my own kids before I ever get my own phone.

"Is that a fancy walkie-talkie?" Eddie gestures to Becca's phone.

"Just my cell phone," Becca says with a shrug.

"You're selling a phone?" Lu looks up from where she's hugging Sandy.

"Not *sell*. Cellular." Becca waves her glittery pink phone. "After my last upgrade it's faster at everything--texting, videos, streaming and games."

"Texting? Videos?" Lu pushes up her glasses. "I don't know what you're talking about but I know that's not a telephone. Where's the dial and cord?"

"Is it a space toy?" Eddie reaches out to touch Leo's phone but Leo draws back indignantly.

"It's *not* a toy," Leo says indignantly.

"Leo is serious about his tech," Becca explains. "You should see his bedroom—it's filled with robotics and computers."

Eddie's brown eyes widen as he stares at Leo. "Your family has a computer?"

"My mother has one," Leo answers. "I have four."

"But computers are bigger than our station wagon." Lu points to the classic car in the driveway. "Dad's a computer technician. He brings home old computer paper and I use it to write my stories. Once Dad showed me the computer at his job and it was as big as a garage. I never heard of a kid with a computer at home."

And I've never heard of a kid who didn't know about texting, videos and cell phones. My crazy suspicion grows stronger.

Sandy whines and rubs her nose against my leg. I reach down to pet her but keep my gaze on Lu and Eddie. There are so many questions I want to ask: *Why haven't we ever met before? Why do your clothes look old-fashioned? How did we get here and where did the freeway go?*

But only one trembling question rises to my lips. "W-What's the date?"

"June 23rd." Lu answers.

"No." My heart quickens. "I mean the year."

"You're a goofy girl." Eddie laughs. "Everyone knows it's 1971."

Leo gasps.

Becca's mouth drops open.

I just stand there, stunned. I suspected we weren't in the 21st century anymore. But seriously? Time travel! How is that possible?

I probably would have stood there forever, freaking out. But the sudden squeal of bike brakes startles me. Whirling around, I stare at a tanned girl with two long black braids. She hops off her bike and runs over to Lu. "Have you seen Rocket?" she asks breathlessly.

"No. Isn't he at your house?" Lu asks, surprised. "Sandy came home so I thought Rocket did, too."

"He didn't! I was sure he'd be back this morning...but he's still gone." The girl's dark eyes shine with tears. "I haven't seen him since last night when he was playing with Sandy."

"He can't be very far away," Eddie says.

"We'll go looking for him." Lu pats Rosemary's shoulder. "Don't worry, we'll find him."

"Who's Rocket?" I turn to the braided girl.

"My dog. He's only eight months old." Rosemary glances around anxiously. "He's really little and has never been gone all night before."

Becca perks up. "What breed?"

"Chihuahua. He follows Sandy everywhere. But Sandy came back last night and-" Rosemary's voice breaks. "-Rocket didn't."

Leo tilts his head and Becca's eyes pool with worry. I know they're remembering the blood on Sandy's paw.

Wherever Rocket is, he's in big trouble.

****

We offer to help search.

Lu loans us her parents' bikes. Mine is so big I can barely reach the pedals.

"My board is faster than a bike." Leo hops on his gyro-board, clicking the remote control.

"Cool skateboard," Eddie says.

"It is not a skateboard, it's the latest in robotic technology," Leo says with a proud lift of his shoulders. "And it can run on solar power so it works anywhere."

Even in the past, I think nervously. If I don't think about the freaky time warp that transported us here, this could be an ordinary pet rescue for the CCSC. So I focus on the missing dog—although I can't help but wonder if he's lost in the past, present or future.

Sandy leads the way, barking excitedly like she's been waiting years for someone to follow her.

We weave through neighborhoods where houses are varying shades of similar with matching mailboxes, classic cars and silver antennas spiking from rooftops instead of satellite dishes. We've traveled a long way from Sun Flower.

Fortunately Sandy seems to know where we're going.

She gallops through streets then cuts through a path in a field. The path roller-coasters up and down hills that rise toward a steep rocky mountain. Could it be Sunrise Mountain? It looks different, though; wilder with tangled oak trees.

"Look!" I roll up beside Leo. "I think that's Sunrise Mountain."

"It can't be." He shakes his head. "The terrain only supports rocks and vegetation. Where are the Sunrise Vista homes?"

"Maybe the question isn't where but *when,*" I guess. "Those fancy houses haven't been built yet."

Leo frowns, clearly at odds with the logic of time-traveling. But we don't talk about it because Becca suddenly shouts, "Sandy tripped and fell in the ditch!"

Everyone stops on the side of the road—except me. When I reach for a handbrake, there isn't one. Instead of slowing, I'm gaining speed!

"I can't stop!" I cry as my wheels spin out of control.

"Pedal backwards!" Eddie shouts.

That doesn't make any sense, but I do it anyway--and like magic my wheels stop spinning.

I hop off my bike and join the others gathered around Sandy.

"Is she okay?" I ask, kneeling beside my friends.

"She whines when she tries to walk," Lu says, kneeling beside her dog. "And she keeps licking her leg."

"I don't see any injuries." Becca gently inspects Sandy's leg. "But there's some swelling so a vet should look at it."

"We can't turn back now," Rosemary argues with a determined glance at Sunrise Mountain. "We need Sandy to lead us to Rocket."

"Sandy isn't going anywhere except to the vet," Lu says with a determined set of her jaw.

Her brother nods. "Yeah, she can't run anymore."

"How will we find Rocket without her?" Rosemary flicks her long braids over her shoulders.

"We'll help you look," I say with a gesture to my CCSC club mates.

Becca gives Lu an encouraging smile. "We're good at finding pets."

"We can utilize the clues I've gathered to locate Rocket." Leo lifts his "evidence" baggie from his vest pocket. He pours out the contents onto his gyro-board: a clump of dark fur, red dirt, a prickly burr and a dried leaf.

Lu pushes up her glasses and gestures to the burr and leaf. "These grow by Muddy Creek below Sunrise Mountain."

I give Leo a "told you so" look at the mention of Sunrise Mountain.

"You go ahead," Lu says. "I'll take Sandy home."

"I'll carry her," Eddie offers, lifting the dog. "You can walk our bikes."

"And we'll help Rosemary look for Rocket," I say. "Leo, Becca and I have found a lot of lost animals. Our club—the Curious Cat Spy Club--is all about helping animals."

"The CCSC has recovered fifty-seven lost pets," Leo adds.

"We won't give up until we find Rocket," Becca says as if making a solemn promise.

After brother and sister leave with Sandy, Rosemary leads us along a narrow hilly dirt road. We ride for what seems like miles until Rosemary stops at a slow-moving stream with dark-green water. "Muddy Creek," she explains.

"It's more of a trickle than a creek." Becca points to the ground. "Look! Two sets of dog prints!"

"Small prints for Rocket and bigger prints for Sandy." Rosemary's voice rises with hope. "The dogs must have run up the Muddy Creek trail." She ducks under a hanging tree branch and gestures to a narrow trail squeezed between dense bushes. "It started as an animal trail but hikers use it, too. It winds to the top of the mountain. It's really rugged so we'll have to leave our bikes and your fancy skateboard behind."

"It's more than a skateboard; it's a gyro-board," Leo says as if offended. "I'll take it with me."

"You can't." Rosemary's black braids sway when she shakes her head. "You'll need your hands free to climb up rocky hills."

Leo lifts his chin stubbornly. "It's an irreplaceable prototype and too valuable to leave behind."

"You sound just like a city kid," Rosemary scoffs.

More like a future kid, I think uneasily.

"Your board will be fine," Becca tells Leo. "Finding Rocket is more important. But we have to hurry before it starts to get dark."

"You have a valid point." Leo sighs as he hides his gyro-board under a dense bush. "We'll need to move quickly. According to my calculations, sunset will occur in 64 minutes. I'll retrieve my board after we find the dog."

If we can find him, I worry as we start up the rugged rocky trail.

Rosemary has climbed the trail before, so she leads the way. And it isn't easy. We jump over crevices and rocks and push through scratchy branches that scrape my arms. It's a steep climb, and after a while my leg muscles burn. I'm breathing hard, but not Rosemary, who leaps over boulders like she's part mountain goat.

When we reach a bend in the trail and Rosemary turns right, Becca grabs her arm. "That's not the right direction. Check out the paw prints." Becca points to tiny paw prints in the reddish dirt. "We go left."

Becca bends over. "There are faint shoe prints, too."

"Probably from hikers or campers," Rosemary explains as we duck under the twisted branches of a creepy dead tree.

"There are mosquitos and poison oak." Leo points to a bush with shiny red leaves. "Why would anyone want to camp here?"

"Because they aren't supposed to," Rosemary says.

I totally understand wanting to bend rules and explore new places. Still I wouldn't want to sleep next to poison oak.

We follow the path to a clearing where the burnt remains of a campfire are evidence that someone was here recently. And they left their trash behind, including a broken glass bottle.

"What slobs!" Rosemary scowls at the mess.

"Littering is horrible," Becca adds angrily.

"And dangerous." I point to a reddish stain on a jagged shard of glass. "Trash is dangerous to animals."

Leo takes a handkerchief from his pocket and uses it to carefully pick up the glass. "Although I lack scientific means to examine this shard, the dried substance appears to be blood."

"Huh?" Rosemary gives Leo a puzzled look.

"Leo is like a walking dictionary," I say with a fond look at my friend. "What he means is that someone cut themselves on this glass."

"Or some *animal*," Becca says with a snap of her fingers. "Sandy had blood on her fur when she came to us, but no cuts. Rocket must have stepped on the glass and Sandy got bloody trying to help."

"My poor Rocky," Rosemary clutches her hands together. "He's hurt and alone. We have to find him!"

"We will." Becca puts her arm around Rosemary. "We came a long way to help Rocket, and we aren't going back until he's safe."

Leo gives me a worried look, and I can tell he's thinking about time travel. How long will we be here? Can we decide when we leave? Or are we trapped here forever? I think of Mom, Dad, my sisters, my brother, my dog and my kitten. Will I ever see them again?

"We have to turn around and look for Rocket somewhere else," Rosemary says, jerking me out of my thoughts. Her shoulders sag. "The trail ends here."

"I disagree." Leo has been walking carefully around the trashed camp, and points to the ground behind the fire pit. "The walking trail may end but the paw prints don't."

I lean my hands on my knees as I bend to look at tiny dark-crimson paw prints. They trail away from the camp and disappear into wild weeds spread towards the cliff.

I choke back a gasp. A terrifying scenario spins in my head. The small dog steps on broken glass, yelps with pain, runs wildly, not looking where he's going and….

My gaze flies over the cliff.

When I glance at the others they're staring at the cliff, too.

Rosemary covers her face and sobs. Becca slips an arm around her. No one speaks. What is there to say? The bloody paw prints say it all. Tears sting my eyes. Why did time bring us here if there was no hope for saving Rocket?

Someone should go over to the edge and look…just to make sure. But no one makes a move. We all know what must have happened…and what we'll see. It'll be hard enough to deal with when we hike back down the mountain.

When Rosemary presses her lips bravely and turns toward the trail, Becca and Leo follow. Sighing, I follow too…then stop.

What was that sound?

I cup my ear, listening carefully. And I hear it again—a faint whine.

Whirling around, I run for the cliff.

Tiny pebbles roll under my sneakers, and I pause to catch my balance. Footsteps thud behind me. I push through tall weeds. When I reach the cliff's sheer rock edge, I drop to my knees and look down.

On a sheer rock ledge sticking out like a pointy chin on the face of the mountain lays a tiny dog. His dark fur is matted with blood and he's as limp as a stuffed toy. He's as still as stone.

Hands brush my shoulders and I glance up at Rosemary.

"ROCKET!" she calls down with joy and terror. "My poor baby! We're here, boy! We're going to take you home!"

But the crumpled dog doesn't move.

"Is he…" Rosemary chokes. "Is he alive?"

"It doesn't look good," Becca says in a hushed whisper.

Leo kneels beside us. "Calculating distance from this ledge and the speed of descent, his landing impact would have been traumatic."

"I heard him whine," I remind Leo. "He has to be alive."

"He is!" Becca jumps excitedly. "His tail is wagging!"

"But he's barely moving and so bloody," Rosemary says, wiping dirt mingled tears from her cheeks.

Becca nods. "He looks like he's in pain and shock. We have to get him out of there."

"But how?" Rosemary bites her lip. "That ledge is narrow and there's no chance for him if he falls off."

"I'll call for--" Becca stops abruptly, frowning down at her shiny pink completely useless phone.

Leo frowns, too, probably calculating the impossibility of a rescue. How can we reach Rocket? When we've helped other animals, we had technology and tools. But Becca can't connect with social media, Leo didn't bring his satchel of drones and techno equipment, and I don't have my spy kit.

We're on our own.

****

No one says anything for long seconds, and the only sounds are whooshing wind and the soft whine of the trapped dog below.

Finally Leo sighs. "The distance to the outcropping is beyond our reach. The most logical recourse is for one of us to return to Sun Flower for assistance."

Rosemary folds her arms across her chest. "I'm not leaving Rocket."

I lift my arm. "I'll go to Lu's house and get help."

"But that would take too long!" Becca argues.

"Approximately 47 minutes," Leo spouts off.

"It'll be dark by then," Becca adds uneasily.

"We have no other choice. I am not leaving without my dog," Rosemary says with a determined look down the cliff. "There's no way to climb down there without a sturdy rope. And none of us is tall enough to reach that far down."

"But maybe all of us are." I snap my fingers as an idea hits me. "We can make a human rope!"

And that's what we do.

Leo calculates our weights and organizes our positions from heaviest to lightest. Guess who is the lightest? Yeah, so I'm the one hanging over the ledge. You'd think I'd be terrified—and I'll admit it's scary—but all I can think about is rescuing Rocket. Despite being trapped and injured his dark eyes shine joyfully. He trusts us to rescue him.

Our human chain must look ridiculous. Becca and Leo hold tightly onto Rosemary's legs while Rosemary holds tightly onto me because she's the tallest and strongest. So I'm dangling like a worm on a hook in the air over the edge of the steep mountain.

Being upside down makes me dizzy. I try not to look down, down, so very far down, to the ground. I force my gaze on Rocket. His little tail is wagging and he has managed to stand on his three of his paws. He limps, not putting weight on his blood-streaked back leg.

I reach for him and my fingers brush across his fur. But I can't get my arms around him. He's too far away.

"Come closer, Rocket," I call softly.

"Can you grab him yet?" Rosemary shouts.

"Almost...almost there...." I say as I stretch my arm.

The human chain lowers me a few more inches, and this time when I touch Rocket's fur, I grab hold.

"Don't be afraid," I say soothingly. "I came a long way to help you. I won't let go of you."

Rocket whimpers and licks my fingers.

I hold tightly to his tiny trembling body.

And in a whoosh of pulling, I'm rising up, up, up.

When I'm dragged back onto the cliff, Rosemary grasps her dog and I sag with exhaustion on the damp weeds. I blow out a shaky breath of relief. Solid ground never felt better!

It takes a minute for my head to stop spinning. Through a blur I watch Rosemary sobbing as she hugs her dog. She's not the only one crying happy tears. I blink mine away then slowly stand and brush the dirt from my jeans.

We did it! I don't understand how we got to 1971 or how Sandy found us. I'm just glad we made it in time to rescue Rocket.

The hike down the mountain trail goes much quicker. Rocket isn't bleeding anymore, and the cut on his leg doesn't look too serious. Rosemary tucks him inside her jacket, a safe cocoon for the bike ride back to her house. She leads us to a blue house almost identical to Lu and Eddie's house, but at the opposite end of the same street.

Rosemary carries Rocket up the steps of her porch then turns back to us with a huge smile. "Thanks Kelsey, Leo and Becca. I don't know if I would have found Rocket without your help. You saved his life. Thank you!"

"You're welcome," Leo says politely.

"We're all about helping animals," Becca says.

I nod, feeling a rush of pride. The CCSC solved another mystery—and for the first time we did it without smart phones, spy drones and the internet.

Rosemary waves. "See you later!"

We all wave back. But I wonder: *Will we see her later?*

I hope not because that will mean we're stuck in the seventies.

There's no time to discuss this with my club mates because I hear a shout and see Lu running down the street toward us.

"What happened?" She pauses to catch her breath. "Did you find Rocket?"

"Yes," Becca answers as she holds the handle bars of her borrowed bike. "He's safe with Rosemary and she's going to take him to the vet. We were just going to your house to return the bikes. How is Sandy?"

"She's fine," Lu says. "My parents just called from the vet. Sandy sprained her leg but it isn't bad and should heal quickly. Come with me back to my house. I want to hear everything that happened."

Lu leads us to a small pink room with book shelves, a small old-fashioned TV, and a wooden dresser covered with glass dog and cat statues.

Becca spots a book titled *Dogs Through History* and flips through the pages. Leo suddenly seems a little awkward, maybe because he's in a girl's room. So I do most of the talking. I tell Lu about the long climb up the trail, the bloody glass shard, and how we made a human chain to rescue Rocket.

"That's super cool!" Lu reaches over to a dresser and pulls out a spiral-bound notebook. She grabs a pen and starts writing.

Leo and I exchange puzzled looks.

"What are you writing?"

"Story ideas. I'm going to be a writer someday and write series like Nancy Drew and Judy Bolton. I want to hear all about your amazing adventure!" Her brown eyes shine behind thick glass lenses as she continues scribbling in the notebook. "Your dog rescue would make a good story. Describe what it was like to hang over a cliff."

"Scary," I say with a shiver.

"It was basic physics," Leo says as he fiddled with dials on Lu's boxy television. "We utilized our combined resources to achieve a rescue."

Lu nudges me then whispers, "Does he always talk like that?"

"Always," I grin. "Sometimes I even understand him. It was his idea to form the CCSC to solve animal mysteries."

She nods, never ceasing in her writing.

Leo taps on the rounded gray-green screen on the TV. "I've seen photos of antiquated televisions, but am unsure how to activate the power. Where's the remote?"

"I thought you were supposed to be smart. You reach out and turn it on." She laughs as she turns a dial. The TV brightens to a black and white picture.

"Oh...of course." Leo's face blushes tomato red.

"So tell me more about your club." Lu turns back to me. "How did it start?"

"We found three kittens that were left to die in a dumpster—we all kept one and I named my orange kitten Honey. We also helped a zorse."

"A what?" Lu pushes up her glasses.

"A hybrid of a horse and zebra: zorse," I say. "You can look online for some cool zorse photos...Oh, I guess you can't."

"On what line?" she asks.

"You'll find out in a few decades." Smiling, I quickly go on. "Anyway, our club has helped a lot of animals. There was a 130 year-old Aldabra tortoise, an abandoned ferret, a lop-eared bunny and lots of dogs. We even met a super hero dog with her own comic book."

"Super amazing! I can already imagine the stories I'll write, starting with the rescue of those three kittens." Lu scribbles fast in her notebook. "Your club sounds so fun! Can I join?"

"Well...that could be complicated," I say, glancing at my club mates.

Becca sets down her book. Leo stops fiddling with the old TV. And I try to think of an answer that doesn't include time travel.

"We wish you could." Becca swoops in for a save. "But we don't live nearby."

"Light years away," Leo murmurs, and I glare at him.

"Oh, I thought you said you lived in Sun Flower. But I guess you're just visiting," she says as if this explains everything.

"Yes, that's it," I say. "Why don't you start your own club?"

"Good idea," she says, brightening. "I'll ask Rosemary and Eddie to join."

"You should," I encourage. "It's an easy and fun way to help animals. We have official club titles—I'm the Spy Tactic Specialist—and we meet at a clubhouse called the Skunk Shack. We ride our bikes around looking for lost pets. We never ask for a reward, but when we're offered one, we donate half to the Humane Society."

"I like that!" she says enthusiastically, flipping to a new page in her notebook. "I've never met anyone like you kids—you're so full of ideas! And you seem different somehow…your clothes and some of the odd things you say."

"We're no different than you," Becca says with her warmest smile.

I nod. "We all love animals and will do anything to help them."

"Well I'm glad you helped Rocket," she says.

"Sandy was the real hero," I say. "She led us here. You're lucky to have such a clever dog."

"Do you have a dog?" Lu asks me.

"Oh yes." I grin. "Handsome is a golden-whip. That's a golden retriever and whippet mix. He's really sweet and loves to play with a Frisbee."

"You should bring him over. I'll bet he'd get along great with Sandy," she says, scribbling more in her notebook. "I know you probably have to go home for dinner, but next time I want to hear all about your animal adventures. You've given me ideas for new stories—a mystery series about helping animals."

I nod but all I can think about are her words "next time." Time is our biggest mystery right now, and I have no idea how to get back home. Sandy led us here, so do we follow her to get back home? But she's already home. We're the ones tangled in the wrong time. I glance over at Becca and Leo and I can tell by their expressions that they're freaking out, too.

How do we get back to the 21st century?

Leo stands. "We should leave."

"Yeah," Becca says, moving toward the door. "It's time to go."

"We hope," I whisper, crossing my fingers.

"I'll walk you to the door." Lu closes her notebook and drops it on her bed.

I open my mouth to say good-bye when my glance falls down on her notebook. It's a plain spiral-bound blue book, but the scrawled name on the cover confuses me.

"I thought your name was Lu," I say, pointing.

"No, that's just a nickname my brother calls me." She laughs. "I didn't get a chance to tell that my real name is Linda."

"Everything has been kind of crazy but I'm really glad we met." I smile as she opens the door for us. "Bye Lu...I mean, Linda."

The sun is just an amber squint in the dusky sky. It's strangely quiet as we slowly walk down the street. My heart pounds and I wonder how we'll get home. Coming here happened in a crazy rush of running. Did we go through some kind of time tunnel by the freeway fence? Could the Myrtle Avenue sign be a magical portal? Can we go back the same way we got here?

As we near the end of the street, I see the Myrtle Avenue sign.

Becca grasps my hand.

Leo grasps my other hand.

"I'm afraid." Becca twists her ponytail.

"Me too," I whisper. "What it if we can't get back?"

"Although suitable geometries of motion in space could support a theory for time travel, I prefer my theory of mass delusion." Leo rubs his forehead. "Or perhaps this entire experience has been an elaborate prank. Time travel is impossible."

But then we hear a bark.

Not a bark behind us, but ahead of us—somewhere beyond the Myrtle Avenue sign.

"I know that bark!" I cry joyfully.

My friends and I run for the sign.

And suddenly a rush of wind grabs me like a giant hand and sucks me into rushing sensations of strangeness. I spin and whirl as if my body is made of air. There's no fear or feeling, only a blur of movement...and then darkness.

When my head stops spinning and my vision clears I'm lying on hard pavement, a wet dog tongue slurping my face.

"Handsome! I don't know how you got here, but I've never been so glad to see you!" I hug my wonderful golden-whip.

I lift myself up by grabbing onto the now faded and worn Myrtle Street sign. Glancing around, I see my friends shakily rising to their feet, too. Leo clutches his gyro-board. Becca reties her leopard spotted scarf around her tangled hair. And our two bikes lie just where we left them, against the chain-linked fence that separates the industrial area from the freeway that rushes by endlessly.

We grin at each other and then hop on our wheels.

Handsome leads the way back home.

The end.

CURIOUS CAT SPY CLUB #1 – QUIZ

1. What hair color streak does Becca have?

2. What is the zorse's name?

3. What does Kelsey call her Grandmother?

4. Name the three kittens.

5. Name Kelsey's childhood sporty friends.

6. What does Leo call his skateboard?

7. What is the name of Kelsey's dog?

8. What kind of animal is Ali Baba?

9. What is Kelsey's favorite classic book?

10. Each kid picked a word for the club name. Which word for which kid?

Tie Breaker!
How many acres does Becca live on?

ABOUT THE AUTHOR

At age eleven, Linda Joy Singleton and her best friend created the Curious Cat Spy Club. They even rescued three abandoned kittens. As a kid, Linda was always writing about animals and mysteries. She saved many of her stories and loves to share them with kids. She's the author of over forty-five books for kids and teens, including YALSA-honored The Seer series and Dead Girl trilogy.

She's also written picture books: SNOW DOG SAND DOG, CASH KAT, LUCY LOVES GOOSEY, A CAT IS BETTER & CRANE AND CRANE.

She's a longtime member of SCBWI and Sisters in Crime, a frequent speaker at schools, libraries and conferences. She lives in the Northern CA foothills, surrounded by a menagerie of animals including dogs, cats, peacocks, horses and pigs.

For photos, contests, writing news and more check out www.LindaJoySingleton.com.

 Linda with an Aldabra tortoise

JOIN THE CCSC

YOUR INITIALS = SPY TITLE

SPECIALTY	ROLE
A. Artistic	A. Agent
B. Brave	B. Brainiac
C. Covert	C. Crusader
D. Dramatic	D. Detective
E. Ecological	E. Expert
F. Forensic	F. Finder
G. Gamer	G. Gumshoe
H. Hi-Tech	H. Hunter
I. Intelligence	I. Investigator
J. Judicial	J. Jokester
K. Knowledgeable	K. Knight
L. Logistics	L. Leader
M. Mechanical	M. Magician
N. Nautical	N. Navigator
O. Observant	O. Operative
P. Poetic	P. Pursuer
Q. Questing	Q. Quizmaster
R. Robotic	R. Rebel
S. Scientific	S. Sleuth
T. Technical	T. Tabulator
U. Undercover	U. Uniocorn
V. Valiant	V. Vanquisher
W. Wise	W. Warrior
X-Z: Create Your Own Title	

A respect for animals can be cultivated at any age.

In THE CURIOUS CAT SPY CLUB three diverse characters solve exciting animal mysteries.

Readers will learn to be responsible pet owners, volunteer to help animal causes, and protect vulnerable animals that have no voice in society.

A list of "Five Ways Kids Can Help Animals" can be found at **www.LindaJoySingleton.com**

CL BVA ZNWE EV OVCW

EXJ GRAY, BVA HAIE YJ N

KVVQ LTCJWQ, IVRDJ

UAPPRJI NWQ RVDJ

HBIEJTCJI. IUBCWK CI

YJEEJT ZCEX LTCJWQI.

Hint: W = N

Each letter represents a different letter.

Made in the USA
Las Vegas, NV
19 August 2021